# PANDORA'S
## RHYME'S REASON

*miss candice*

# CONTENTS

# REMINDER

Each book in the Pandora's series is a novelette (short story)

# QUOTE

"...the file never told the whole truth. Just the black and white version. Just the shit that they are obligated to tell. Age. Kinks. Do's. Don'ts. Shit like that. But everyone has an underlying reason for joining..."

**– SAINT BAPTISTE**

# Judah

SHE WAS NERVOUS.

I could tell by the way she maneuvered through the crowd. Confident, but unsure. Unsure because she felt out of place. I'd been watching her since she walked in an hour and... I took my eyes off of her to put them on my Rolex. An hour and twenty-five minutes ago. I'd been sitting at the bar, just... watching her. Couldn't help myself, to be honest. She was captivating in every sense of the word. Captivating in a way that separated her from the rest. It wasn't her beauty that kept my eyes on her; she wore a mask. A red one, speckled with rhinestones and a feather. I was initially drawn in by the way the red mini dress melted into her curves—but that wasn't what kept my eyes on her. She was magnetic. But that magnetism wasn't even it. She had *this thing*. A sway in her hips that separated her from the rest. An *awkward* confidence that had likely gone unnoticed by the plethora of men she'd turned down. To them, her confidence was bold. But to me... it wasn't. It was forced. Not too much though. It was subtle.

She had a sway in her hips that separated her from the rest. The awkwardness I mentioned earlier? Lived there. *It* was in the sway of her hips. The way she walked told me she didn't wear heels often. She didn't *own* them. She chose heels because she thought she needed them to add sex appeal. She didn't; she'd ooze it without them. She was sex appeal. She didn't need to do much. I couldn't see her eyes. Couldn't see her face. But I knew... just by that awkward confidence that underneath that mask, she was striking. A rarity. A diamond in a sea of cubic zirconia's.

Why?

Because she didn't belong here.

That awkward confidence told me a lot. She was nervous. She was new and the only reason she'd *stepped into* Pandora's box was because she was invited inside. It wasn't the invitation that brought her inside though —she answered because Pandora's was needed. Pandora's was an anomaly; I couldn't imagine there being another place on earth quite like it. People came here to have their wildest, deepest, and sometimes darkest fantasies fulfilled. Some came to watch. Some came because their sexual appetites were rather... peculiar. And then... there were women like her. The ones who ventured off onto the dark side and found themselves in the underworld. That's what Pandora's was for real —the underworld. A world outside of the real world and that was why women like her ended up responding to invitations inside. Not because they had a fetish— but because they hadn't been fulfilled so they came here looking for sexual satisfaction.

"Doing it again?" Asked Lee, the bartender who'd been replenishing my 1942 all night.

I lightly snickered and looked away from the lady in red. "Doing what?"

"Giving people a story," she stated before resting her arms atop the bar. She nodded in the direction of the mysterious woman and asked, "What's hers?"

I smirked, picked my glass up and finished it off before putting my eyes back on the lady in red. "She's new."

Lee nodded. "*Okay?* Don't tell me that's all you've come up with. Nigga, you've been sitting here for—"

"Married with children. A stay at home mother with an aggressive appetite," I disrupted. I ran my tongue over my bottom lip and added, "She's looking for something specific."

"And let me guess," Lee said with the suck of her teeth. "You?"

I glanced over at her with a cocky smirk. "Nah. Not *me*." With a grunt, I paused. "What I have to offer, yes."

She rolled her eyes, twisted her lips up and pushed away from the bar, after someone called for her. "Mmhmm. Anyway. She's a freak, Judah. That's it. A freak who's simply trying to bust a nut. Like every other freak in here . You love to get philosophical and shit." She giggled. "She might be new but she's looking for the same thing every other bitch in here is looking for: dick. Nothing special. Just a nut. She can get that anywhere. *You* just want to be the one to give it to her so... you've convinced yourself that you're the man for a job that any one of these niggas can do."

Right after she said what she had to say, she walked away. Good. She didn't know what the fuck she was talking about. We weren't here just because we were 'freaks' as Lee had disrespectfully claimed. Lee's perception was tainted because of the way I handled her. Because I fucked her a few times and lost interest, she thought that was just the way things went here. She hated when my attention was on someone other than her. She was jealous. What she wanted was for me to get philosophical about her ass. But I wouldn't. Hadn't. She wasn't interesting enough.

The lady in red was. Lee was wrong about her. She was always wrong about them. We did this often. Well, not as often as I would have liked. Pandora's, my drug of choice, hadn't housed anything as interesting as Red in months. On a rare occasion, someone would catch my eye. Whenever I found prey, Lee would notice and talk shit. She'd ask me to tell her the story I came up with, I'd share my thoughts, she'd say some hating shit, swear I was wrong, and walk off. Because I wasn't the kiss and tell type of nigga, I never told her how right I'd been. About every last one of them.

So, as *Red* made her way through the crowd, I knew I was right about her. Women were predictable. The only thing that always caught me by surprise was pussy. *Pussy was my forte.* It fascinated me. Its uniqueness. There weren't two pussies alike. I've had a couple that looked the same but there was always something vaguely different that separated one from the other. The taste. The feel. The grip. Pussy was magnificent.

As Red strutted through the club, heading in the direction of the elevators, I ogled her, boldly sweeping my eyes along every inch of her, wondering what hers would feel like. I wondered... if it was dainty. Wondered if she was a creamer, or a squirter. Or... if she was a as much of a rare gem as I depicted her to be. She looked to be full of surprises.

If she was a creamer, tonight I'd make her both.

And if she was a squirter... tonight she'd cream. I had intentions to make Red feel in ways she'd dream about until the day she died. I wanted tonight to be cemented into her memory. She wouldn't be able to touch or see her pussy without thinking of what I made it to.

She noticed me staring but pretended not to by looking in every direction but mine. She did that a few times since I noticed her. Evaded eye contact, shied away... Mmh.. I couldn't wait to get my hands on her.

5

There was something about that good girl, hard to get, timid shit that drove me insane.

When she stopped at the elevator, pressed the up button and stood there, with her hands clamped in front of her, my interest was piqued further.

After fishing a few bills from the pocket of my tan slacks, I tossed them onto the bar top and walked off, deciding that I'd wasted enough time watching.

"Leaving?" Lee asked, busy tending a customer.

I nodded. "Hell yeah. Prey on the move." With a smirk, I chucked my chin, bidding Lee a good night and walked off with my eyes planted on 'Reds' ass.

Because the elevator was a nice little distance from the bar, I had to put a little pep in my step. But shit, I could only move so fast. It was Friday—one of the busiest day of the week at Pandora's and the place was crowded as hell. Couldn't move around without bumping into someone or something. Just as I'd made it through, she was on the elevator and the doors were closing.

"Ay, hold the do—"

Before I could tell her to hold them, they closed. I was sure she heard me. The subtle smirk I noticed just as they met in the middle gave it away. She didn't want to be bothered. Or did she? Felt like she wanted this. Like she wanted me to chase her, so I would. Either I was bugging, imagining shit, or I was just that good at reading women. Regardless of if she wanted me to chase her or not, I intended to. Never in a million years did I think I'd be chasing a woman in a club full of women, but I was.

I hit the up button, stepped back, and watched where the car would stop before it made it back down to me. Eleventh floor. Hmph. She did have a preference. She was particular. She was here looking for something specific. The eleventh floor though? Nah. She couldn't be. Dominate? With *women*? Nah... there was more going on. Had to be. Shit just didn't add up.

With pinched brows, I looked away and waited for the car to come back down. Shortly after, I stepped on and was immediately enveloped by the scent of lavender and vanilla. *Damn*, she smelled good. I rested against the glass wall with my hands stuffed into the pockets of my slacks, head tossed back, eyes closed, wondering if she'd taste as good as she smelled.

The short ride up to the eleventh floor was spent thinking of a lot of things. Visualizing, really. Before I laid with a woman, I spent a great deal of time fantasizing. Not only about the act of sex but every single thing that would lead up to it. Sex was an art. To me, it should be treated with the respect. The body of a woman, especially.

The elevator sounded and I stepped off. The eleventh floor was like a completely different world from the ones below and above. There wasn't a level in this building like the eleventh floor. There were many spaces here that led to destinations most muthafuckas couldn't even *dream* of. Pandora's was the epitome of fantasy . Anything you could think of Pandora's could give it to you. I'd had my share of fun. Had spent a lot of time behind each door in the building. I had my limits though. Didn't get too crazy. My preference was pussy, and pussy only. Anything outside of that spectrum, I didn't fuck around with it. Pegging and shit included. Pussy was my forte. Remember? My appetite for it was *aggressive*. Women were masterpieces. Couldn't imagine my dick getting hard for anything other.

So.

If it was pussy in a room, I'd explored the depths of it.

Literally and figuratively. Tonight, I came with the intention to explore several. However, the minute I noticed her, there was a change. I only wanted to explore hers.

Once I made it to my destination, I looked up at the security camera and waited to be granted access. It didn't take long for the doorman, Nino, to open up.

Standing back, I held my arms out for him to check me although I'd already gone through a checkpoint upon entry.

"Red mask. Curly hair. Lavender and vanilla. Will I find her inside?" I asked.

"You know the protocol, nigga," Nino flatly responded before stepping aside with his arms crossed over his broad chest. "Have a good night though."

His eyes stayed forward. Stare remained pensive, ignoring me.

"I thought I knew protocol. Since when Princess's come through the front—"

"Have a good night, nigga," Nino reiterated, this time, with his beady eyes locked on mine.

I nodded and carried on, with every intention to have that good night.

I'd been a platinum member at Pandora's for about seven years and with it I could explore every inch of the building. The membership came with a ton of amenities. However, it didn't give me immunity. I couldn't breech protocol. The NDA we were required to sign didn't just protect us outside of the building—it protected us all, inside of it too. Questions about members were off limits. And while Nino was cool, he was a no-nonsense type of nigga. I knew he wouldn't give me shit. But I said fuck it and tried anyway.

*She couldn't be a dom.*

That didn't fit the plot. She was timid. Her confidence was quiet. Awkward. *Shit*, she could barely walk in heels. She wasn't a dom. She didn't fit the profile. Fuck no. I *needed* her to be on the other side of the field. For this to work... for tonight to go the way I needed it to go, she had to be. But she'd been here. She came through the same doors I entered. Nino didn't have to tell me shit.

That lavender and vanilla lingered in the air. Carried down the rest of the hallway and died out at a door marked **RESTRICTED**. I stood there a moment, staring at it with a racing heart. My mouth salivated and I closed my eyes as I brushed my hand over the gold handles. Thought of her rushed through my frontal lobe and my dick *immediately* bricked.

Soon, my hands would caress her. Soon, I'd have my hands wrapped around her. Soon, it wouldn't be her scent in the air, exciting me. It would be her taste. I couldn't—

"*Judah*," Nino barked. "Carry yo' weird ass—"

"Aight nigga," I interrupted with a grunt.

Weird.

Was I weird? Naaah. *I* didn't think so. I was a student, studying the lady in red. I knew exactly what I was. Fixated. And that made her lucky. I had a tendency to fixate on things. Women. Not things... *just women*. Beautiful women. Women I desired. When I found someone to fixate on, I was relentless. When I said sex was an art, I meant it. I was an artist and the body of a woman... my canvas. I was intentional with the way I handled them. Each brush of my fingers across their magnificent skin was delivered with the type of passion they required. And they all required something different. Just as much as there weren't two pussies alike, there weren't two women with the same desires. That notion, 'if you've fucked one, you've fucked them all', was silly nigga shit. Rookie nigga shit, really. If a nigga had that type of mindset, it meant he hadn't given them what they required. He was lazy. He was a piece of shit who didn't know the first thing about pleasure.

I adjusted my tie, cleared my throat, and stuffed my hands into the pockets of my blazer before turning to continue down the long hallway to the door that would grant me access to her. I stood there a moment and brushed the pad of my thumb along the engraved lettering of *'Pandora's Princesses'*.

Mmmph.

The lady in red...

A princess. I would have never guessed *that*.

# 2

# *Rhyme*

"YOU READY?" ASKED GISELLE, WITH HER HEAD BETWEEN the crack in the door.

No, I wasn't ready. I didn't know what the hell I was doing. But, I was doing it. For the past three months, I'd pretty much been on autopilot, just... doing shit. Things that didn't make any sense to *me*. But made a great deal of sense to the part of me that needed *'this'* most.

Cupping my breasts, I looked over my shoulder. "My drink? Did the girl bring—"

"Oh yes! She just walked in. *Oneee* second," Giselle excitedly interrupted before disappearing back behind the door.

I took a deep breath and turned back to face the mirror.

Giselle was my 'handmaid' for tonight. Handmaid.

What in the hell did I, Rhyme Reynolds, need with a handmaid? Well.. tonight, I wasn't Rhyme. Tonight, I went by Jezebel, and Jezebel needed a handmaid because '*she'd*' signed up to be a Princess at Pandoras and every princess had a handmaid.

What's Pandoras? Same question I had when I found an invitation addressed to me, inviting me here two months ago. It was a normal day. I was leaving the grocery store when I found an envelope tucked underneath my windshield wiper. The sunlight hitting the gold, iridescent envelope beckoned me to open it right then. There was something about it. I wasn't only drawn to it because it was beautiful. When I said I was beckoned, that's exactly what it felt like. There was this indescribable pull toward it. Normally, I would have been alarmed to find a suspicious envelope addressed to me, on my windshield but for some odd reason, that day I wasn't. The minute I opened it, the normal day I thought I was having, flipped. Normal would have been me piling my groceries into the trunk, and then driving home with music I shouldn't have known word-for-word on full blast.

But... I found an envelope.

Addressed to me. Beautifully addressed to me, might I add. It was the finest piece of stationary I'd ever laid eyes on, let alone gotten my hands on. And it was for me. Initially, I thought it was a wedding invitation. It didn't occur to me that it had been placed suspiciously. I didn't think anything of it really. I thought, hey maybe someone recognized my car in the parking lot and decided to drop it on my windshield. Shit, I didn't know. Who's first thought would have been sex club? Not mine. I wasn't wired to think that way and didn't know anybody who was. So, when I read it and saw that it wasn't an invitation to a wedding, but a sex club instead I was very taken aback. Confused and... slightly offended. Who would invite me to a sex club? I lived a very reserved life and didn't dabble into anything remotely close to what the invitation entailed.

However, those feelings of confusion and disrespect were short lived. I did a quick scan of the parking lot and tucked that little invitation right into the inside pocket of my Telfar. After hurriedly piling my groceries into the trunk of the car, I got inside, pulled the invitation back out, and dialed the number at the bottom of the page. I was curious and honestly... a little excited. Should have been afraid but, I was tired of being afraid. I'd lived most of my life afraid, doing the *right thing.*

After the call, I still wasn't one hundred percent in. I drove the fifteen minute ride home contemplating on what to do. And when I finally did make it home, I locked myself in my office and made a list. I weighed the pros and cons. I was one of *those people*. Careful. I drew a line down the middle of a sheet of paper and scribbled about why I shouldn't and why I should take the trip downtown to Pandoras. There was only one reason why I should, and about twenty on the side of why I shouldn't. Obviously I went the other way because although the scales were severely imbalanced, the latter *still* outweighed the other.

My first night was exciting. I didn't do anything. Just... watched and impulsively purchased a yearly membership. The invitation was for one night only but after I walked inside and 'felt' Pandoras, I decided that one night just wasn't enough. The building was packed and there was so much going on. So much sex. So much... sin. All of the action excited me. How could it not? Pandora's was a place to be free. A place to let go and just be without limits.

Inhibitions didn't exist here. Walking inside gave me chills. A feeling of euphoria... this rush of freedom. The weight of being Rhyme Reynolds lifted as soon as I pushed past the big steel doors. Who I was on the other side of them... Who I was before I crossed the threshold, died. There was something exhilarating about checking in that I wanted to feel again. And again, and again. As I stood at the check in desk, I decided that one time wouldn't be enough. I had to feel that freedom as often as possible. So, I did something crazy... I purchased a platinum membership. It was steep. Too steep, but I purchased it anyhow. I never did anything nice for myself. I deserved it.

*Anyway*... that's what landed me here... in a Princess suite. *Well*, not exactly.

When I joined, I told myself I'd take advantage of

every single thing Pandoras had to offer. I had a list. I wasn't supposed to explore the eleventh floor until the final day. But... earlier I found myself in a game of cat and mouse that urged me to move floor eleven up my list.

*Knock. Knock.*

A second later, Giselle reappeared with my martini and my hands found my breasts again. She handed me the glass with a smirk. "How do you expect to stand in that room naked and you can't stand here, in front of me, without covering your nipples, Jezebel?"

Jezebel was the name I used here. There was a line for aliases and... well... Jezebel seemed to be fitting. Right? I was here to be a whore, wasn't I? I hadn't been. Not yet. I planned to be. I planned to live up to it so much that once I got to the end of my list, I'd have years' worth of repenting to do.

"I'll do *just fine*," I said with a wink before tilting the glass to my lips. "Trust me."

I was a different person when I was in character. I wasn't Rhyme when I was on the floor. She died and Jezebel came alive. Jezebel held her head high, shoulders back, and had a certain sway to her hips. She wore lavender and vanilla, short dresses, spandex, thongs, and bejeweled masks. Jezebel could, confidently, stand naked for a room full of men.

I swallowed my drink down and turned my attention to the mirror. Shifting my eyes between my legs, I lightly sighed. Well... I hoped I would be able to.

Giselle crossed her arms over her chest and slightly cocked her head to the side. "You say that now. Here and there are completely different spaces. Here and the floors below, completely different worlds. You still have time to back out if—"

"I'm not backing out," I interrupted. "Thank you, Giselle but I'll be fine. There are safe words and such, right?" I joked.

She lightly giggled and nodded. "Yes, there are. But," she stepped forward. "Understand that being a Princess isn't one dimensional. It isn't like what you see on TV and read and books. Some of the dynamics aren't even about sex and—"

"*Giselle*," I breathed out. "Are you about to go into The Gallery, or is it me?"

"I'm just saying, I'm just saying. It's your first day and—"

"I know what I'm doing."

She pulled her lips into her mouth before saying, "No, I don't think you do." She paused and sighed. "If I'm overstepping any boundaries, please let me know. I'm just—sweetie, you don't belong here. What are you doing here? Why are you here?"

"Because I can be," I flatly told her. "Please," I nodded toward the bottle of body oil seated on top of the vanity. "Get my back for me?"

She took in a deep breath, nodded and grabbed the bottle. "You know... nothing surprises me about this place anymore. However, this... tonight... *you*... you've surprised me."

I smiled a little. It was subtle. So subtle that I was sure she didn't notice. Hearing that I'd surprised her sent a chill down my spine. I didn't hear that often. In fact, I didn't hear it at all. I was predictable—as Rhyme. I had a routine. There was nothing spunky or witty about me. nothing unique. I did what I was supposed to do. Smiled, paid tithes, prayed, obeyed the law... I was a good girl. In every sense of what it meant to be a good girl. But... being the good girl got boring.

When Giselle said I didn't belong here, she didn't mean I *literally* did not belong at *Pandora's*. she was speaking about my membership and how I wasn't supposed to be *here*—in one of the Princess penthouse suites preparing to serve, when I should have been getting served. She was right. I didn't *belong* here. But, I wanted to do it all. Platinum members didn't typically sign up to be Princesses but with my membership I was free to do whatever the hell I pleased.

About ten minutes later, my dark brown skin was glistening and bare as the day I was born. My eyes shifted down to the bush sitting between my legs again, and I swallowed. I was insecure about a lot of things, but here in this setting, I was insecure about my bush the most. In today's society, where pussy's are preferred balled, I was sporting a full 'fro down there. I wanted to shave. Even thought about getting a wax...*but I couldn't*. If I did that...

Anyway...

I hated it. So much that the bush was the reason I hadn't done anything but watch since joining. I was afraid to be seen. Afraid that if someone saw me, they would judge, and I wouldn't be desired. I was a beautiful woman. I had a couple of flaws—skin wasn't the clearest, and I could stand to lose a few pounds, but other than that, I was very attractive. I'd heard I was beautiful all my life. There had been plenty of men here who'd tried to get between my thick thighs, but I turned them all down. Not because I *wanted* to. I didn't pay thousands of dollars to join just to watch. I wanted to feel as well, but.... that insecurity crippled me.

So, why in the hell did I think it would be a good idea to stand in a room amongst other beautiful women, ass naked for men to choose from? Did I think that through? Not really. Actually, I didn't think it through at all. It was him. He had me all jumbled. Threw me completely off. Made me lose my marbles damn near. On the upside, maybe this was the push I needed to get the engine running.

"You look delicious," Giselle flirted, standing directly in front of me. Her eyes started to travel down the length of my body, and I immediately covered my 'hoo-ha' with my hands. She stepped forward, gripped my wrist and lightly pulled them away. "You can't do that in there. This is your final chance to pull out. Would you like me to have your profile extracted from the ballot?"

Our eyes stayed locked for a few seconds.

My heart raced and my lips parted. I wanted to say yes. Wanted to tell her to tell them never mind. Wanted to pull out of this foolish game of cat and mouse. What in the fuck was I doing anyway? I had no business here. Had no business playing games with anyone. Especially not someone like him.

"Okay I'll have them—"

"No," I blurted out.

Shoulders back.

Head high.

Pussy on full display. *Hairy pussy* on full display. Damnit Rhyme.

Giselle smirked. "Alright then." Pausing, she continued. "If it isn't inappropriate... can I say something?"

We walked off, in the direction of the door.

I giggled. "Something more inappropriate than saying I look delicious?"

She laughed and shrugged. "*Wellll*... you do. But no. Nothing *crazy*."

"Go ahead."

Giselle opened the door and gestured for me to walk out. "Stop hiding yourself. You're beautiful. Every single thing about you. That bush especially. It separates you from all of the other pussy's out there. I don't see bushes anymore. Just landing strips and Brazilian's." We walked out into the hallway, and she added. "You know what it gives? Vintage. Classic. *You* give classic, Jezebel. It's sexy. Own it."

Did I want to be vintage? Did I want to *give* classic? In a space filled with women who were... modern? With weaves down to the cracks in their asses. Big asses too. Big, BBL asses. While I stood there with dints and cellulite? They were slim thick. Whereas, I was just... thick, thick. Not thick. Chubby. That's what I'd heard all my life. I was chubby. Didn't fit under the category as thick because I had a pudge. It was subtle. Just a little bit of cushion but it was there. And standing there, ass naked, with every flaw on display... around them... with my natural hair and subtle make-up... I didn't feel as confident as I did before I made it to the Princess Penthouse. These women were... shit. Breathtaking. Social media pretty. I was west side of Detroit, suburban pretty.

But pretty still.

Good enough, still. Bush and all.

Giselle made me feel a little better about my bush. Besides, I didn't want to look like everyone else. I was okay standing out. I was in a line of twenty-something women, being escorted to a white room, with a bright light to be scrutinized by only God knows how many men. And... I felt good.

The walk down to the room was quiet. Giselle stayed back, while who I assumed was the head mistress, lead us down a long hallway to *The Gallery*. The only sound that filled the space was the sound of my own heart racing and heels clacking against the marble floors. I was a nervous wreck.

"Remember... eyes forward, chest high, shoulders back," The headmistress stated before grabbing hold of two golden door handles.

Seconds later, I was standing in that white room with my not so perky 38DD's extended, shoulders pulled back, five foot seven inches, two hundred and fifteen pounds, that made me, me on display. And I wore my vintage bush with confidence. Well, a little bit of liquid confidence. That martini was slowly but surely working its way through my system.

It was quiet. Intimidatingly quiet. My heart raced as I stood there, listening as every number was called but mine. I was eleven. That liquid confidence slowly dissipated the longer I stood there, waiting to be picked. I felt humiliated. I wanted to run. Wanted to hide. Never wanted to show my face at Pandora's again.

Where was he?

I thought he was interested.

Well... Maybe he was. Until he saw what was hidden underneath the dress. Until he saw the bush. Maybe he saw me for me and decided, nah... she's not it. Maybe I wasn't what he truly desired. Before, I wore a masquerade mask. Maybe he wasn't into full lips, a lightly wide nose, and almond shaped eyes. Did I really think he'd choose me? After seeing *them*?

I was the last woman standing. Like a fucking fool. Like that unappealing cheap ass cluster ring at the jewelry store. I felt... *desperate*. I swallowed and my shoulders dropped just a little. I was tempted to turn and just leave but I couldn't do that. I couldn't show them, or him, how defeated I was. I had to stand tall. Had to remember my why. Had to remember... that this place... me coming here... it wasn't about him. It was about me. I didn't come here for one man. I just so happened to catch the eye of one I really fucking liked and... so what if he didn't like me after seeing me for me? Feelings didn't belong in Pandoras. They couldn't be hurt. I had to push through the shit.

"11," said the head mistress over hidden speakers. "Please make your way to the corridor."

It was over. Had to be. I hoped so. I didn't want to be the woman who was chosen last. I didn't want to be settled for.

Once I made it to the corridor, I was slightly disappointed to learn that I was indeed chosen last. I was greeted by a security guard who introduced himself as Slim. But he wasn't. Slim I mean. He was big. Linebacker big. He rambled off a few guidelines as he led me out of the corridor through another set of double doors. He talked the entire walk down to the room.

"Like I said before, don't forget to use your safe word. Newcomers tend to forget," he paused and looked over at me with a stern expression. "Don't."

I swallowed as the gravity of what I'd gotten myself into began to settle in. What if it wasn't him? What if it took so long because he did see me and changed his mind about me? What if the little game of cat and mouse I thought I was playing ended a long time ago?

Did he even follow me up here? Did he even know I was—

"We're here," Slim stated, interrupting my thoughts. He stood at the door, pulled a matte black keycard from the pocket of his vest, and waved it above the doorknob. After there were two beeps, he opened it, stepped aside and let me by. Nodding he said, "Have a good night. Don't forget what I said about the safe—"

"You're leaving?"

He shook his head. "I'm not. You're safe. I'll be right here."

Slim rested against the matte black wall and crossed his arms over his chest. I nodded at him and turned my attention to the gold door. I stood there a moment with my head slightly cocked over to the side, staring at it. Not just because I was nervous to walk inside, but because there had been a flip in design. Every door I encountered here had been black with gold hardware. Except this one. This one was gold with black hardware. Interesting.

After a couple of seconds of standing there, Slim cleared his throat. I glanced over at him, took a deep breath and finally walked inside.

The room was immaculate. Nothing like what I expected. I thought I'd walk into a dungeon. Something with whips, chains, and all kinds of kinky shit. But, no. It was the complete opposite. The room was bright, with white walls, and furniture too. It was almost as bright as The Gallery. The light wasn't as blinding. It was subtle. Comfortable. I'd never stepped foot in a room as luxurious and... peaceful as this one. I was confused. Taken aback really. I thought the purpose of all of this was for pain. I thought that as a 'Princess', I would be a submissive, and whoever, a dominant. Maybe there were a few things hidden behind the closed doors. Probably some type of contraption that would come out of the ceiling.

There was a huge, California King sitting in the middle of the room, covered with white silk bedding. Sitting on top of it, just at the foot, was a sunflower. Next to it, a red blindfold. I assumed it was for me? I came out of my heels, and slowly advanced toward it, my bare toes sinking deeper into the white plush, sheepskin rug the bed sat on. First, I picked the sunflower up and brought it up to my nose and inhaled with a smile. I bypassed the blindfold and ran my hands over the bedding as I rounded the bed, taking in the rest of the room. Shifting my eyes over to the massive cream colored drapes covering the floor to ceiling windows, I decided to take a peek out.

Damn.

I had a *perfect* view of Downtown Detroit. I had Birdseye view of the people mover, and Woodward Ave. It was breathtaking. The lights from the buildings, the traffic, and everything in between. It was busy. I wasn't used to seeing so much action. It was quiet where I lived and not nearly as lively and bright. I stood there for a while, just... watching. I was in amazement, as I watched the many cars zip up and down the roads. It was fascinating really. The reality that everyone had somewhere to be. The reality that there were so many people in the world just... living. And there I was, on the eleventh floor of Pandora's a secret little sex club not too many people knew about. But... I knew about it. I felt elite. Like I was truly apaprt of a secret society. I felt superior. I didn't feel superior often. But as I stood behind the thick glass window, overlooking Downtown Detroit, ass naked, I did. And you know what? My confidence began to rise again. I was—

"Good evening."

I flinched, startled and snapped back to reality.

For a second, I slipped. I got so wrapped up in *where* I was that I forgot *why* I was here in the first place. Had even forgotten about my little dilemma. The chances of *him* not being my dom. I needed to turn around. But if I turned around, and it wasn't him, I would be crushed. My heart would drop down to the bottom of my ass, and I'd see then that I had truly bit off more than I could chew. It had to be him. Right? I tried to register the 'good evening' to the voice of the man who'd called for me to hold the elevator earlier but, couldn't. He wasn't close enough before. I... *shit*.

Oh God. What in the hell was I thinking? If it wasn't him—

"You good?"

He was closer. Standing right behind me. He hadn't

26

touched me, but I could *feel* him. Either he was dangerously close, or his presence was as thick as I thought it would be. It had to be him. I hadn't felt a presence as thick as his since I stepped foot in this place.

If it was him or not, I had to turn around. Couldn't just keep facing a damn window like some weird person. I mean... all I'd have to do was say my safe word and I'd be safe and if he didn't honor it I was sure Slim would intervene. He couldn't be outside of that door for nothing.

Taking a deep breath, I finally turned around.

And lightly smiled.

It was him.

And my God was he gorgeous up close. From a distance, through the distortion that my mask created, I could only take in so much. Then, he was just tall, light skin, and handsome. Now, standing just inches away from my lips, he was gorgeous. Breathtaking. And *he* chose *me*. Took him long enough but... his fine ass chose me. I didn't get chosen often. Well. I never put myself in a space to be chosen. Well then again, I never really had to. What was, was and I was content with that. Not anymore though. Hadn't been for quite some time. This month was just my first time actually doing something about it.

"Hi," I spoke. "I—I saw the blindfold and I was going to put it on but then I noticed the windows and I—"

"It's cool, love. *Fuck that blindfold*," he interrupted as his eyes bore deeper into mine.

I swallowed and drew back a bit. Well... damn. I thought his stare before was intimidating but I was wrong. This was intimidation. This stripped me. Made me vulnerable. Well, I was always vulnerable. Always... 'weak'. But with liquor in my system, I shouldn't have been. I should have been able to turn it off. Should have been able to 'turn up'. I wasn't supposed to care about being naked. Wasn't supposed to care about being exposed.

But he stripped me.

Of the liquor, and the courage it gave me too. Hell, he stripped me of Jezebel.

I looked away from his pensive stare to calm my nerves, but he gripped my chin and turned my head back in his direction. Our eyes locked again, and I was rendered speechless. He had this thing about him. A way that made me want to shy away and draw in closer to him at the same time.

He stepped back and my hands immediately went to that 'v' between my legs to hide my bush. *You're classic, Jezebel. Vintage. It's sexy. Own it,* Giselle's words ran through my mind. Own it, Rhyme. There is nothing wrong with—

Before I could give myself the courage to move my hands, he stepped forward, grabbed my wrists, and lightly pulled them away. "Don't hide."

I shook my head. "I'm sorry. I—"

"You're not sorry..." he interrupted before stepping back to 'examine' me. That's what it felt like. Like I was being examined. Like I was back in The Gallery, waiting to be selected. Especially when he circled me. I stood there with my arms at my sides, stiff as a statue. I was so nervous that I had to remind myself to breathe a few times. He stood behind me, brushed my curls from the side of my neck and whispered into my ear, *"You're exquisite."*

# 3

# *Judah*

SHE WAS NOTHING LIKE WHAT I IMAGINED.

She was better. Everything about her was. The way she felt. The way she smelled. The way she tasted. Every fucking thing. And to think... I'd almost missed out on my opportunity to have her. I was almost a minute too late. I stood in The Viewing Room, over-looking The Gallery just... watching. Transfixed on everything that she was. Meticulously, I did a very slow sweep of every single inch of her. Had I not been fixated on her, I would have heard the bidding war brewing behind me. When more than one person wanted the same Princess, there was an auction. I didn't prepare for an auction. Not because I didn't think she was desirable enough, but because the minute I laid eyes on her downstairs, in my mind, she was already mine.

The wager was steep. Up thirty-thousand. Just as

Marcellus, one of the niggas bidding on her, was about to pull out, I snapped out of my zone. Right on time. Had I been a minute too late, I would have lost her to this sick ass nigga with a scat fetish. Colin's pockets were steep—but so were mine. He had a cap—I didn't. Not when I was fixated on someone. I didn't place a bid unless I was fixated and tonight... my fixation ran deep.

I took thirty thousand to sixty and as expected, Collin tipped his hat and bowed out.

I didn't regret my decision to double it. Not one bit. If I had to, I would have tripled it. Shit, quadrupled it. She was... *delectable*. And I hadn't even made it to her pussy... yet. I'd get there... however, I wanted to wait. The pussy was a treat; tucked nicely behind a *thick* bush of hair.

"What's your name? Your real name. Not the lie you put on your profile." I asked, before lightly gripping her neck to turn her head to kiss her on the side of the neck.

"Rhyme," She confessed.

That was easy.

I didn't think she'd give it to me.

"Why did you pick Jezebel? Are you a whore, Rhyme?" I asked in between kisses, as my right hand made its way up her inner thigh.

She shivered a little and gripped the silk bedding. "No, I'm not a whore.

I looked up at her. Her eyes were closed. I told her

31

to open them. She listened. She was a very good girl. However, I felt like she only listened because she thought she was supposed to. Because she had a misconception about how this between us went. Soon, she'd see. Soon, she'd learn that this dynamic, *here*, was *gravely* different.

"You see that?" I whispered into her ear, steady inching my hand up her thigh.

"See what?"

"You."

There were mirrors on the ceiling. I had quite a few suites on the eleventh floor, but I selected this one *specifically* for her because I wanted her to see herself completely free. I wanted her to see what true bliss was. I wanted her to see the exact moment in which she was there. She wouldn't be able to capture every single moment—I didn't want her to—but that first one was most important. She'd see it *whenever* she closed her pretty little brown eyes.

"Mmhmm," she mumbled as soon as I made contact with that bush she was so got damn self-conscious about.

Subtly, she pulled her knees together, and softly, I pushed them back into position. "Mm, mh. Stay open for me, gorgeous. And... keep them pretty ass eyes open too. Don't you fuckin' close them."

"Okay, *sir*—"

I stopped. Pulled my hand back, sat up a bit and

blocked her view of the mirror. "We don't do that here."

"We don't?" She asked through labored breathing, with dipped brows.

God, she was so fucking beautiful. I didn't find beautiful here. Sexy, fine... shit like that. But this woman? This woman was fucking beautiful. It was her innocence. That awkward confidence. The fact that she'd chosen a silly ass name like Jezebel. She was no jezebel. I knew that the minute I spotted her. She really, truly did not belong here. She was *too much* of a rare breed. I'd be lying if I said I wasn't glad she hadn't stumbled inside though.

"Not *here* we don't," I sternly told her.

"I don't know how this goes. I thought I was supposed to call you sir and there would be whips, chains, bondage and—"

"Is bondage what you desire?"

It wasn't—but I asked anyway. I knew exactly what she needed.

"I'm here to serve you; I desire whatever you desire."

I paused again and simply stared at her. Got a little lost behind her brown eyes. "That's not the way this goes neither, *sweetheart*."

That explained a lot. She was obedient only because she thought she had to be. Her perception was skewed. Or was it mine? I didn't play by the rules. I did what I wanted to do. Rhyme wasn't here to serve me. She was *my* princess—*I* was here to serve *her*. I wanted to make her feel good. I wanted to do whatever she wanted me to do. This wasn't about me. This was about pleasing her. And in pleasing her, I would give myself great pleasure. She was at Pandora's for a reason and well... I wanted her to leave tonight, fulfilled. That was my purpose—to fulfill Rhyme's needs. To give her what she hadn't been given.

The situation wasn't typical. Didn't fit the *standard* dominant-princess narrative. And that was because I wasn't typical, and I didn't play the role of a 'dominant'. I didn't *play* the role of anything. I was the fuckin' pussy whisperer.

I ran the back of my fingers across her cheek, and she leaned into my touch. Delicately, I gripped her chin and turned her to face me again. I then lowered my lips to hers and kissed her. When our lips met, she moaned into my mouth and wrapped her arms around my neck. She deepened the kiss. Met me with aggression. But I stopped her, pulled back and told her to slow down. I didn't tell her, but I didn't want to rush. Not only because I wanted her to enjoy the night. Not only because I wanted it to be unforgettable for her, but because I wanted it to be unforgettable for me as well.

Rhyme was a diamond.

A red diamond.

Rare. Very hard to come by. I was sure that after tonight, I wouldn't be able to step foot into this place without thinking of her. Wouldn't be able to stand in

The Viewing Room without placing her in it. Wouldn't be able to stand in the elevator without closing my eyes, inhaling and fantasizing about her scent. Wouldn't be able to put my mouth on another woman without first thinking of her bush, and then her taste second.

Despite knowing that tonight would be our first and only night, I hoped that it wouldn't be. Women like her—who chose silly names like Jezebel and had a quiet, awkward confidence when it should have screamed—didn't color outside of the lines often. Hope couldn't exist in a space like *this*, with a woman like her. So, as our tongues did the tango, I made sure to make it a dance she—no... we would remember.

She moaned into my mouth when I lightly sucked on her tongue.

Everything about the fucking woman was sexy.

There wasn't a thing about her that I hadn't found to obsess over. She was classic. She was that piece of art people went to galleries to stare at for hours. Just to marvel over. Simple but... mesmerizing. The black Mona Lisa.

"How does it go then?" She whispered, once I pulled away from the kiss to devour the rest of her.

I didn't respond. I didn't have to. I wasn't a talker. Didn't like to talk about the things I would do—would rather show.

My only response was a subtle kiss to her chocolate chip sized nipples. She was pleased with that; the way she arched her back told me so. Every time I touched her, her response was heightened. Every little stroke of my hands across her skin. Every time my lips touched her, she responded as if I'd penetrated her. every touch had been innocent. We hadn't made it past second base, and she was quivering.

I wondered; how long had it been since she'd been touched?

Fuck touched... how long had it been since she'd gotten what *she* desired? Rhyme had been neglected. She was feverish. Hungry. The kiss told me so. The way her body responded to me told me so. This woman... this beautiful piece of art... hadn't been cared for properly. She'd been in the wrong hands. It was aight though... tonight, she was in my hands, and I planned to take very, very good care of her.

I made a trail of kisses from her nipples down to that bushy V. I felt it the minute she tensed. I paused and looked up at her. Those eyes were closed again.

"Rhyme," I called out.

"Hmm?" She answered through labored breathing.

"Eyes on that mirror, baby," I told her, as I sifted through her garden.

She gasped once I lightly pinched her clit. It didn't take me long at all to find it. Did she think it would? Did she think this would scare me? *Shit*... this excited me. I'd been with plenty of women... more than I could count... and not once had I experienced a pussy like

36

hers. Full. Womanly. Beautiful. That's what it was to me.

"Mmmh," She moaned when I started to move my fingers back and forth over it.

The longer I toyed with it, the harder it became, the more she squirmed.

"Mmhmm. Keep them eyes open, love," I told her, as I kept my eyes on her.

She was the focus. Would be until the night ended. Until she was exhausted and drained of every bit of pussy juice she could muster up. I wanted her to leave Pandora's completely exhausted. In a good way. I wanted her walking on legs that felt like wet noodles out this bitch.

She nodded and moaned. "Mmkay. I—I will. Oh my...wha—"

I stopped. Pulled away just as the furrow in her brows deepened and she began to buck her hips a little too much. She was close. Too close. I didn't want the first one to be like that. I wanted that first one to be on my tongue. I wanted her to drown me. Because I knew she would when it happened, I didn't want to waste it. I wanted to ride the tidal wave. Wanted to be submerged in it... wanted to be carried by the current.

"Patience," I mumbled, before leaning forward a bit to rub my nose against her pulsating bud.

She moaned.

Bucked her hips.

Gripped the sheet.

"Eyes open," I told her.

Couldn't see her but I knew they were closed. It was almost as if she was afraid to see herself. I wondered if it was shame that forced her to shy away. Wondered if she thought of him... the world outside of this world... while I laid between her legs. If that were the case, that was aight. She could think of him. She was allowed to worry. She could be shameful. After the first one, she wouldn't be. After the last one, she would think of me whenever she laid with him, and whenever she wasn't. She'd think of me, *always*.

"Okayyy," she whined.

"Good girl."

I kissed her clit, and she groaned. Whimpered a little. Her pussy was sopping wet. She was a creamer. Her bush was speckled with white. Reminded me of those chocolate cream filled cupcakes. Mmmh. I hadn't eaten one since I was a child but tomorrow, I planned to stop by the store to grab a box. She was... drenched. My mouth salivated. I wanted to dive in. Wanted to dip my tongue inside. But... I had to practice patience too.

However, I couldn't help myself.

I dipped my tongue inside. Just... the tip of it before I then dragged it back up to her clit where I gently sucked.

"Mmm," I groaned, as her taste teased my tastebuds, making me greedy.

I knew better. I knew the first taste would only make me want more. *But shit...*

I gripped her thighs, slightly digging the pads of my fingers into her skin, and ate her pussy with *precision*, savoring every swipe of juice that touched the tip of my tongue. I didn't rush. I took my time. Gave her slow, deliberate strokes. Her moans were like music to my ears. In my hands, she quivered, squirmed, and jolted and I loved every fucking second of it.

Her pussy grew sweeter just as she was at the brink of cumming.

I looked up. And as expected her eyes were opened and on that mirror. She was mesmerized. Her hands had found her nipples. Her mouth laid agape, as she swirled her hips, pushing her pussy deeper into my face. I welcomed it. She was close. Her face wore the sexiest expression of bliss I'd ever witnessed.

"Mmmhmm," I purposely hummed into her pussy to create vibrations that would take her right over the edge.

She didn't moan—she yelped. Screamed. She took her hands from her nipples and placed them on the back of my head. I gripped her by the waist and pushed my face deeper into her pussy, hummed and lightly sucked on her clit.

"Oh my Goddddd," she cried and violently shook, as that first one washed over her.

My beard was *drenched*. She was a creamer. But she was a squirter too. Tonight she was. For me. Her pussy wouldn't do that for anyone else. I was sure of it... would bet every fuckin' dollar to my name on it.

One she finished her eyes met mine, and I stayed there for a minute. Slowed down and gave her clit soft kisses before I sat up and positioned myself between her legs, on my knees.

I gripped her by the waist and slid her down the bed. "You're not here to serve me—I'm here to serve you," I mumbled, rubbing the head of my dick on her glistening clit before slowly sliding into her.

# 4

# *Rhyme*

I DIDN'T WANT TO LEAVE BUT THE SUN WAS RISING. I wanted to stay forever. Not only because last night had been the best night of my life but because it felt good to just... be. To exist in a space where I could be completely free. But places like Pandora's only existed for the escape. I'd escaped. I'd gotten what I needed. It was time for me to go back into the real world. A world where I didn't exist as Jezebel. A world where I existed as Rhyme Reynolds. A name that held a lot of fucking weight. A name that would carry more weight once I stepped out from behind the black steel doors that separated fantasy from reality. I had a lot to carry tonight. Well... *today*... this morning.

I didn't know how I would exist as Rhyme after experiencing *him* as Jezebel. I didn't want there to be separation. I wanted to mesh the two. Intertwine them the same way I was intertwined with him. He was awake. Holding me, as if we were lovers instead of strangers who'd only met hours ago.

"You good?" he asked, cutting into the silence... *cutting into my fantasy.*

"Yes," I said with a light giggle before turning over on my back. "I'm... great, actually."

I stared where a ceiling should have been. There were mirrors. And God we looked good. I couldn't imagine actually sleeping under something like this. I wouldn't get a wink of sleep, but it was nice for Pandora's. Pandora's wasn't for sleeping. It was for fucking. And mirrors were built into ceilings for the purpose of watching the fucking. I didn't do much of that. I did enough of it. Saw what he wanted me to see. But eventually the focus shifted to just... us. And he let it. We were in sync for most of the night, engrossed by one another instead of the mirror. But now, after bliss had settled, I was finally able to appreciate the beauty for what it was. Beauty that was the two of us. We were like... those ice cream cones. The kind that mixed. Chocolate and vanilla. Soft served. Stuck together, sweet. Double the treat. We... we meshed well.

Here.

Couldn't imagine us working anywhere else.

We wouldn't.

We couldn't. Even if there was a possibility... we couldn't. Jezebel only existed here. I was Rhyme. The one with a life. A real life. separate from fantasies. Separate from spontaneity.

A real fucking life.

I turned away from the mirror at the feel of his soft lips against my sweat dampened skin. "Did you find what you were looking for?" he asked, cutting into my thoughts again.

I looked back at him with pinched brows. "Hm?"

He pulled himself up and sat against the headboard. "What you were searching for here... what drew you in. Did you find it? Are you satisfied?"

For some odd reason, his question triggered me.

Shit. Shit. *Shit.*

I looked away as tears began to swell behind my brown eyes. Before he could notice, I immediately sat up and wrapped the soft silk sheet around my body, *hiding.* For what? He'd seen, touched, licked, kissed, and sucked nearly every inch of me.

*I was satisfied.*

I had gotten what I needed.

Intimacy. I didn't come to Pandoras searching for intimacy. I came here looking for sex. But he gave me intimacy in a place I didn't think intimacy existed. I hadn't been touched like that in... *never.* I thought it was passion I needed. But what I got was what I *truly needed...* and from a man who didn't even know me.

Snorting, I looked over my shoulder at him and nodded with a coy smile. "Yes, Judah. I did." I bit down

43

on my bottom lip and got a really, *really* good look at him. He looked at me the same way I looked at him. Deep. With a sigh, I added, *"Thank you."*

He nodded with a smile. "My pleasure."

We sat in silence for what felt like minutes but couldn't be more than a couple of seconds before he nodded towards the bathroom. "Would you like to join me?"

Pulling my lips into my mouth I nodded. *"Yeah, Sure."*

He was a Godsend, really. Either he didn't want our moment to end just yet, or he could sense my hesitation and wanted to do me the favor of granting me more time.

THE THIRTY MINUTE drive to the hotel room I was supposed to be at last night was spent thinking of him. He bathed me. When we got into the shower... he grabbed a bath sponge and *bathed* me. He was delicate and showed extra special attention to every inch of me —not just my 'private parts'. He was calculated. He was precise. He was... everything. After experiencing that... after experiencing him, leaving was harder. I shouldn't have showered with him. I should have gotten up and left right at that instance, but I didn't and now I was left with more memories. More reasons to go back. I didn't want to. I needed to. But... at the same time, I didn't need to because I couldn't exist here and there. I couldn't split into two. Pandora's was no place for a woman like me. I had to snap out of it. But how was I to? After what he did to me? After what he gave me?

He didn't just *give me* intimacy. He 'gave me' a nice amount of money too. Apparently, it wasn't always a bad thing to be picked last. Usually it meant that there was an auction, and the stakes were high. Last night was the highest grossing auction Pandora's had ever had. He thought I was worth sixty thousand dollars. I was baffled. Last night didn't seem real. Nothing about it did. I didn't get the full sixty—I left with fifty percent but still... sixty thousand *for me*? How was I supposed to carry on with my life as if nothing happened, after *all of that*?

I wouldn't be able to. Once I settled into my room, I showered again. Tried my damnedest to scrub 'last night' off of me but all I could think about was him and what I'd done. All I could think about was what would happen when I got home. I was riddled with guilt, shame, and... desire. I was a fucking mess. I had never in all of my thirty-four years experienced a level of intimacy anywhere close to that. He handled me as if he loved me, and I responded as if I loved him too. That wasn't just sex. That wasn't just a one night stand. He kissed me. Deep. Held me after. We showered together and the man bathed me. That was passion. That was... intimacy.

HOURS LATER, I was rested enough and turning into the subdivision of my home. As soon as I did, my racing heart picked up and I twisted the steering wheel. For some silly reason, I thought that when I woke up, I would feel better. Today's return from my 'staycation' felt different. There was a ton of guilt on me. Usually, I'd be able to shake it off. Today, there was no shaking. No letting it go. No forgetting. Last night would stay with me forever. And as great as it was, I didn't need that. I wasn't sure if I'd be able to handle it.

When I pulled up in front of my home, I took in a deep breath and decided not to open the garage. I needed another moment to get myself together before I stepped completely into the role of Rhyme Reynolds. So, I shifted the car into park and sat in the driveway with my head tossed back against the headrest with my eyes closed.

Tasha Cobbs, *Break Every Chain*, played at a low-level, as I took a couple of deep breaths.

"*Mommy!*" My eyes shot open at the sound of my daughters voice.

She was at my window with a bouquet of red roses. I killed the engine, unbuckled my seatbelt and opened the door to finally get out of the car. Before I could get out, Arionna enveloped me in a big hug, and I bombarded her chubby little cheeks with kisses!

I was a mother. Had two children. A little girl and boy. Five year old twins. Arionna and Aaron. *Rhyme* was a jezebel; Rhyme was a homemaker.

"I missed you!" She shrieked.

"I missed you too, honey bun. Where is your brother?" I asked.

"In the kitchen with grandma. They got—"

"Let mommy get out of the car, Ari."

"Okay daddy!" Ari yelled before unwrapping her arms from around my neck. With a laugh, I watched as she ran off into the house, carrying the roses she was supposed to give me. Busy body.

Looking away from her, I smiled at my husband, Andre, standing in the doorway with his arms crossed over his chest. He wore a smile *almost* as big as Ari's. I wasn't *just* a mother. I was a wife, too, and had been for ten years. Andre and I were teenage sweethearts. We grew up in the same church. Andre was the only man I'd ever been with. He was my other half. He truly completed me. Last night was magnificent but was it good enough to throw away a lifetime of love? Absolutely not. We had our issues, but those pro's still outweighed the cons.

Sure, what Judah gave me, Andre couldn't and that was... *okay*. I needed it to be. For years it had been okay... until it wasn't. Until I needed more. Until I found myself literally starving for something more. Something more than just a quickie. Or something more than just... sex with nothing else attached to it. Dre and I had been together for so long that sometimes I wasn't even sure if he truly desired me. Sometimes it felt like he didn't even see me. I felt invisible until he needed me for *something*.

"Hey doll," Dre greeted with a kiss to the forehead. "How was your night?"

I smiled and wrapped my arms around his waist. To avoid his eyes, I laid my head on his chest and decided to listen to the sound of his heart. "It was great. I feel... good."

He grabbed the sides of my face and pulled me away from his chest. "You *look* good. Happy."

I smiled and quickly kissed him on the lips before pulling away to pop the trunk. "How was your night? Did you get anything done?"

Andre walked over to grab my duffle bag from the trunk. "It was good," he responded before closing the trunk. "Mom stayed over and helped with the kids. I got a lot done." We walked up to the house, side by side. Andre draped his arm over my shoulder and pulled me closer before dropping a kiss on top of my head. "Tomorrow's service is going to be fantastic. God willing."

I wasn't asking about work when I asked if he'd gotten anything done. I was asking if he'd gotten anything done around the house. Or if he'd spent any quality time with our children. But in true Andre fashion, his only concern was the church and perfecting his sermon. Andre was a preacher so naturally, as cliché as it might sound...I was more than just a wife, I was a *preachers* wife.

Andre's father was the preacher at Mount Zion Baptist Church, the church we grew up in. Naturally, Andre followed in his footsteps and me, in *his* mother's footsteps. I didn't plan to live a life of fellowship and worship, but it was the life I kind of stumbled into because I just so happened to fall in love with Andre. For the first few years, before we got married and he stepped into his father's shoes, things were blissful. Things were exciting. We took trips. He showered me with love and good sex. But still, there was no intimacy.

Andre treated me like a cum rag and I mean, I was okay with that. It wasn't until I found questionable text messages between him and Sister Kendra last year, that I decided I needed more. They seemed innocent, but he had no business talking at one o'clock in the morning. I asked him about it and apparently she was going through a crisis, so he snuck out of bed to pray with her. I didn't buy it. Dre never gave me a reason to think he was cheating. I thought I had a good man. He was a man of Christ for crying out loud, but since then things had been at a steady decline.

It took that to happen for me to realize just how long I had been severely lacking. And not *just* in the sex department. In the *everything* department. Dre didn't have time for anything but the church. He poured into it more than he poured into me. It felt like since we had gotten married the only role I was to play was that of a helper.

Once that invitation showed up on my windshield, I figured I'd go out and get that excitement I so badly desired, myself. After practically begging for biweekly 'staycations' he finally okayed them. But with the stipulation that I'd return on Saturday afternoon to prepare for service on Sunday. I was alright with that. I just... I needed something. But realistically, I needed more time. After my first night at Pandora's I realized that. It wasn't just about Pandora's neither. I needed more time for me in general. More time away... more time to just be. I was drowning. Suffocating here. Suffering. But because I knew I was ways away from longer 'staycations' I settled and looked forward to my biweekly trips to Pandoras. However, after last night I wasn't sure about going back. I was afraid that if I did, and I saw *him* again I'd slip further away from reality and into that fantasy and I *couldn't* do that.

"Hey mommy!" Aaron spoke, colliding into me once I walked into the house.

The way my kids greeted me, you'd think I was gone for a week instead of one day! The love filled my heart with a type of joy that nothing else in the world ever would. If there was a reason not to go back to Pandora's it would be because of them.

"Hey baby boy! I missed you. Look at you; what is that on your shirt?" I asked, taking a good look at him.

He giggled. "We cooked! Come on mommy!"

He grabbed my hand and pulled me, dragging me out of the foyer, through the living room all the way to the kitchen where my mother stood at the island over a breakfast feast. There were pancakes, waffles, cinnamon rolls, bacon—both turkey and pork, eggs, grits, skillet potatoes, fruit... just about everything!

"Hey, Rhyme, baby," greeted my mother with a big smile as she undid her apron and rounded the island to meet me with a hug. We embraced and she asked, "Did you enjoy your night away?"

"Yes, ma, I really did," I said before we pulled away from the embrace.

We locked eyes and her smile widened. "That's very good to hear." She then gripped my hands and whispered. "You're glowing."

My eyebrows furrowed. "What do you—"

"Come on! Look at all of this food we made, child!" She interrupted with a wink. "You know, I've been slaving over this stove since five while *Pastor Andre* did nothing?"

"Aw come on now, ma! I was in and out." Dre yelled with his hands up, guilty as ever.

"Mmhmm! With your dirty little hands in my bacon! You ain't lifted one finger."

I giggled. Tried to act normal but there was something in my mother's tone that told me she knew.

Either she just had that mothers instinct, or she was the one who'd given me that invitation. Since receiving it, I hadn't thought much about where it could have come from. I didn't really care too much. I should have but desperation wouldn't allow it. Plus, I felt safe in my mask. Didn't roam without it. But... if my mother gave me that invitation—

"Stop thinking so much," she whispered, nudging me in the side. "*You're glowing.* Appreciate the glow." She paused and looked over at me. "I sure do—I was waiting for it."

The invitation came from her. It had to.

My mother had me at sixteen. I was raised in the church *with her*, by my grandmother. She, like me, grew up religious however she had a rebellious spirit. The invitation coming from her didn't cross my mind once. But as I stood beside her, in the kitchen with my family, preparing to have a breakfast feast, it made sense. Perfect sense. I had a ton of questions but decided to just let it be. Besides, did I really want to talk about sex with my mother? I didn't. I'd rather just carry on with my life as if the last five minutes didn't happen.

"I bet he was in here digging in the food, ma. He's good for that. Always ready to eat, never wanting to help!" I joked, jumping in on the conversation.

"Nun uhn! Daddy helped!" Aaron added. "He got the roses!"

I looked down and Ari pushed the roses toward me.

"He did? Well, they are beautiful!" With a smile, I looked over at him. "Thanks, daddy."

Dre walked over, wrapped his arm around my waist and kissed me on the cheek. "You're welcome, baby."

I was grateful for this.

For family. Despite how rocky things were, I really was.

And, I was grateful for Judah... and the courage it took for me to step inside of Pandora's. Growing up, I'd always heard bad things about 'pandora's box'. Pandora's box got a bad rep. It was always used to heed warning. But... no. Since signing that contract life only seemed to get *better*. If you were from *this* life, you wouldn't see it that way. Pandora's would be seen as a sin because of all of the unholy things that happened there, but it was more than just that. It was a place people went to embrace their true selves, and to experience bliss like never before.

Pandora's, although a bit wild, was a little piece of heaven tucked away in hell. I couldn't imagine settling... after experiencing that feeling of euphoria that rushed through my veins every single time I crossed the threshold. I wouldn't settle. Refused to. Especially not after experiencing *him*. I was afraid, yes. But fear had stopped me long enough, hadn't it? I owed my children more. And despite our issues and my suspicions, I owed Dre more, too. But what about Rhyme? Didn't I owe her the most? I just... I had to find balance. That's what Pandora's was about too. Finding balance. A balance between true self, and the parts we kept hidden away from the 'real world'.

Pandora's was a mystical, beautiful place where fantasies and desires came alive.

And I couldn't wait to go back.

THE END

## AUTHOR'S NOTE

I hope you enjoyed the first installment to the PANDORA'S series. I had a ton of fun writing it. I know, I know... You want more. Unfortunately, this is where Rhyme's story end. However, you *will* see more of Judah throughout the series.

Thank you.

*Miss Candice*

Made in the USA
Monee, IL
22 July 2024